Dear Deer

Dear Deer

A Book of Homophones

GENE BARRETTA

HENRY HOLT AND COMPANY

New York

A NOTE TO THE READER

Homophones are words that sound the same but are spelled differently and have different meanings, such as *moose* (the animal) and *mousse* (the dessert). *Homonyms* are words that sound the same and are spelled the same but have different meanings, such as *bowl* (a round dish) and *bowl* (the sport).

Henry Holt and Company, LLC
Publishers since 1866
175 Fifth Avenue, New York, New York 10010
www.henryholtchildrensbooks.com

Henry Holt® is a registered trademark of Henry Holt and Company, LLC.
Copyright © 2007 by Gene Barretta
All rights reserved. Distributed in Canada by H. B. Fenn and Company Ltd.

Library of Congress Cataloging-in-Publication Data
Barretta, Gene.
Dear deer: a book of homophones / Gene Barretta.—1st ed.
p.   cm.
Summary: When clever Aunt Ant moves to the zoo, she describes the quirky animal behavior she observes by speaking in homophones, from the moose who loved mousse to the fox who blew blue bubbles.
ISBN-13: 978-0-8050-8104-6 / ISBN-10: 0-8050-8104-6
[1. Homonyms—Fiction. 2. Zoo animals—Fiction.] I. Title. II. Title: Book of homophones.
PZ7.B275366Dea 2007   [E]—dc22   2006031369

First Edition—2007 / Designed by Laurent Linn
Printed in the United States of America on acid-free paper. ∞

10 9 8 7 6 5 4 3 2

The artist used watercolor on Arches hot-press paper to create the illustrations for this book.

For my Deerest Leslie (I'm still fawning)
and all my special Ants: Jane, Kathy, Elaine,
Caroline, Dot, Dee, Sandi, Norma, Josie

—Love, Gene

DEAR DEER,
I now live at the zoo. Wait until you **HEAR** what goes on over **HERE.**

Love,

AUNT ANT

The **MOOSE** loves **MOUSSE**.

He **ATE EIGHT** bowls.

Have **YOU** seen the **EWE**?

She's been in a **DAZE** for **DAYS**.

That's **HIM**, the **HORSE** who is

HOARSE from humming a **HYMN**.

It's quite a **FEAT** when the bat
hangs from his **FEET**.

The monkey will tell
you a **TALE** as he
hangs from his **TAIL**.

The **DOE KNEADED** the **DOUGH**,

because she **NEEDED** the dough.

The **TOAD** was **TOWED**

to the top of the seesaw,

so he could **SEE** the **SEA**.

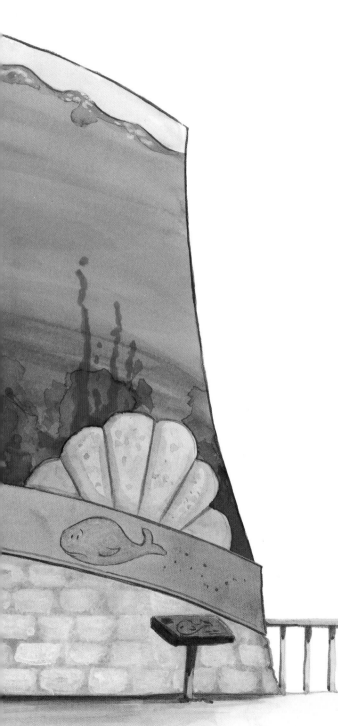

The **WHALE** was **ALLOWED**
to **WAIL ALOUD.**

The **BEAR** had to **PAUSE**

to **BARE** his big **PAWS.**

HEY, the elephant **THREW** a pail

THROUGH the big bale of **HAY!**

Have you **READ** about the **RED** fox

who **BLEW BLUE** bubbles?

The giraffe's long neck
lets him CHOOSE
what he CHEWS.

The cows in the **HERD**

were in a good **MOOD**.

I HEARD them as they

MOOED in harmony.

The bee **FLEW** away from the flea with the **FLU**. And the **BEE** can **BE** sure that if he had the flu the **FLEA** would **FLEE**, too.

There is no **NEWS** about the **GNUS**.

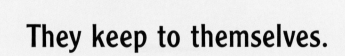

They keep to themselves.

AUNT ANT,

You do have some very interesting new neighbors. I have a new neighbor, too! Do you **KNOW** about the **HARE** with **NO HAIR**? She's an expert on skin care.

Love,

Your **DEAR DEER**